PUFFIN BOOKS

UK | USA | Canada | Ireland | Australia | India | New Zealand | South Africa

Puffin Books is part of the Penguin Random House group of companies
whose addresses can be found at global.penguinrandomhouse.com.

www.penguin.co.uk   www.puffin.co.uk   www.ladybird.co.uk

Penguin
Random House
UK

First published 2018
001

Characters and artwork are the original creation of Tove Jansson
Written by Richard Dungworth
Text and illustrations copyright © Moomin Characters™, 2018
All rights reserved

Printed in China
A CIP catalogue record for this book is available from the British Library

HB: 978-0-141-37559-5
PB: 978-0-141-37560-1

All correspondence to:
Puffin Books, Penguin Random House Children's
80 Strand, London WC2R 0RL

FSC
www.fsc.org
MIX
Paper from
responsible sources
FSC® C018179

MOOMIN
and the
Ice Festival

BASED ON THE ORIGINAL STORIES BY

Tove Jansson

PUFFIN

*I*n *M*oominvalley, the first soft flakes of snow were falling.

Inside *M*oominhouse, the *M*oomin family were preparing for their Long Winter Sleep.

"Pee-hoo!" yawned *M*oomintroll as he helped *M*oominmamma move the beds around the big drawing-room stove.

Little My was too busy to help. She was hunting her pet house-spider, which had escaped – again.

Snorkmaiden burst into the room, full of excitement. She was clutching a handbill.

"It's an invitation!" she gasped.
"To the Ice Festival!
Tonight!"

Snorkmaiden's big eyes shone as she pictured dancing and elegant dresses.
"May we stay up and go this year?" she pleaded.

"If it's all the same," Moominpappa said
wearily after a busy day of fastening
shutters and draining water tanks,
"I'd prefer to stay where we're warm
and comfortable."

Moomin's feelings on the matter were somewhat muddled. The Ice Festival sounded exciting, but to go outside now winter was here . . .

"It might not be safe," he told Snorkmaiden. "What if we meet the Groke?"

Snorkmaiden's tail drooped and she left the room.

"Poor dear!" said Moominmamma. "Still, I think Pappa is right. And we all need our Sleep."

"Stick-in-the-muds!" snapped Little My. "If you never go out in winter, how do you know it's so terrible?"

With that, she scampered away after Snorkmaiden.

That evening, when Moominmamma rang the supper-bell, neither Snorkmaiden nor Little My answered its call.

Moomin trotted upstairs to fetch them.

Snorkmaiden's room
was deserted.
Tummy aflutter, Moomin
peered outside and found
a rope-ladder dangling from
the open window.

A double set of footprints led away
across the blanket of moonlit snow.

Moomin raised the alarm.
"They must have set off for the Festival!" he told his parents. "What if they get lost? We have to go after them!"

At the scent of adventure, Moominpappa rallied. "A rescue mission, eh?
That's the ticket!"

But he couldn't help but think of the
cold, grey Groke.

"That's enough of that," he told himself sternly.
"I must be brave." Snorkmaiden needed him.

The trail climbed through a shadowy forest.
Moomin's heart quickened. His ears pricked at
every noise – then he heard a faint tinkling sound.
"Music!" said Moominpappa.
They pressed boldly on . . .

and found themselves at the edge
of a frozen lake. Its banks were lined
with gleaming lanterns.
"The Ice Festival!" gasped Moomin.

Out on the ice, a high-spirited group of valley folk were skating, feasting and making merry.

Moomintroll scanned the crowd for his missing friends.

"Bless my tail!" cried Moominpappa.

"It's Too-Ticky!"

Their old friend was accompanying the ice-dancing on her tinkling barrel-organ.

Then Moomin's heart leapt. There, at last, was Snorkmaiden – gliding along, looking more beautiful than ever, a winter rose tucked into her hair.

Little My was zigzagging before her.
Moomin rushed to join them – and was
soon having the time of his life.

As midnight approached, the shimmering
Northern Lights filled the sky. Moomin
and Snorkmaiden oohed and aahed.
Snorkmaiden thought Moomin
very heroic for coming after her.

"It was Little My's idea to sneak off," she said sheepishly. "And I did so want to come."

"Quite right too," smiled Moomin. He was cross only with himself, for almost allowing his fears about winter to let him miss this magical night.

The homeward trip was downhill all the way
– and a wild, exciting ride!

"Wooo-hooo!"
whooped Little My.
"Faster! Faster!"

At the Moominhouse, Snorkmaiden presented Moominmamma with her winter rose.

"Sorry," she said simply, nose flushing.

"How lovely!" smiled Moominmamma.

"You should have seen the Northern Lights! And the skating!" said a still-excited Moomin.

"And so she shall," promised Moominpappa.

"At next year's Festival."

Moominmamma heard all about the Festival before steering her family to bed for their Long Winter Sleep.

"You'll hear Too-Ticky's barrel-organ again soon, when she plays it to welcome the spring," she told Moomin softly as she tucked him in. "And won't that be lovely, my Moomintroll?"

But Moomin, happy, cosy and full,
was already fast asleep.